PARABLES OF A
PROVINCE

GILBERT PARKER

PARABLES OF A PROVINCE

THE GOLDEN PIPES

They hung all bronzed and shining, on the side of Margath Mountain—the tall and perfect pipes of the organ which was played by some son of God when the world was young. At least Hepnon the cripple said this was so, when he was but a child, and when he got older he said that even now a golden music came from the pipes at sunrise and sunset. And no one laughed at Hepnon, for you could not look into the dark warm eyes, dilating with his fancies, or see the transparent temper of his face, the look of the dreamer over all, without believing him, and reproving your own judgment. You felt that he had travelled ways you could never travel, that he had had dreams beyond you, that his fanciful spirit had had adventures you would give years of your dull life to know.

And yet he was not made only as women are made, fragile and trembling in his nerves. For he was strong of arm, and there was no place in the hills to be climbed by venturesome man, which he could not climb with crutch and shrivelled leg. Also, he was a gallant horseman, riding with his knees and one foot in stirrup, his crutch slung behind him. It may be that was why rough men listened to his fancies about the Golden Pipes. Indeed they would go out at sunrise and look across to where the pipes hung, taking the rosy glory of the morning, and steal away alone at sunset, and in some lonely spot lean out towards the flaming instrument to hear if any music rose from them. The legend that one of the Mighty Men of the Kimash Hills came here to play, with invisible hands, the music of the first years of the world, became a truth, though a truth that none could prove. And by-and-by, no man ever travelled the valley without taking off his hat as he passed the Golden Pipes—so had a cripple with his whimsies worked upon the land.

Then, too, perhaps his music had to do with it. As a child he had only a poor concertina, but by it he drew the traveller and the mountaineer and the worker in the valley to him like a magnet. Some touch of the mysterious, some sweet fantastical melody in all he played, charmed them, even when he gave them old familiar airs. From the concertina he passed to the violin, and his skill and mastery over his followers grew; and then there came a notable day when up over a thousand miles of country a melodeon was brought him. Then a wanderer, a minstrel outcast from a far country, taking refuge in those hills, taught him, and there was one long year of loving labour together, and merry whisperings between the two, and secret drawings, and worship of the Golden Pipes; and then the minstrel died, and left Hepnon alone.

And now they said that Hepnon tried to coax out of the old melodeon the music of the Golden Pipes. But a look of sorrow grew upon his face, and stayed for many months. Then there came a change, and he went into the woods, and began working there in the perfect summer weather; and the tale went abroad that he was building an organ, so that he might play for all who came, the music he heard on the Golden Pipes—for they had ravished his ear since childhood, and now he must know the wonderful melodies all by heart, they said.

With consummate patience Hepnon dried the wood and fashioned it into long tuneful tubes, beating out soft metal got from the forge in the valley to case the lips of them, tanning the leather for the bellows, stretching it, and exposing all his work to the sun of early morning, which gave every fibre and valve a rich sweetness, like a sound fruit of autumn. People also said that he set all the pieces out at sunrise and sunset that the tone of the Golden Pipes might pass into them, so that when the organ was built, each part should be saturated with such melody as it had drawn in, according to its temper and its fibre.

So the building of the organ went on, and a year passed, and then another, and it was summer again; and soon Hepnon began to build also—while yet it was sweet weather—a home for his organ, a tall nest of cedar added to his father's house. And in it every piece of wood, and every board had been made ready by his own hands, and set in the sun and dried slowly to a healthy soundness; and he used no nails of metal, but wooden pins of the iron-wood or hickory tree, and it was all polished, and there was no paint or varnish anywhere; and when you spoke in this nest your voice sounded pure and strong.

At last the time came when, piece by piece, the organ was set up in its home; and as the days and weeks went by, and autumn drew to winter, and the music of the Golden Pipes stole down the flumes of snow to their ardent lover, and spring came with its sap, and small purple blossoms, and yellow apples of mandrake, and summer stole on luxurious and dry; the face of Hepnon became thinner and thinner, a strange deep light shone in his eyes, and all his person seemed to exhale a kind of glow. He ceased to ride, to climb, to lift weights with his strong arms, as he had—poor cripple—been once so proud to do. A delicacy came upon him, and more and more he withdrew himself to his organ, and to those lofty and lonely places where he could see—and hear—the Golden Pipes boom softly over the valley.

3

At last it all was done, even to the fine-carved stool of cedar whereon he should sit when he played his organ. Never yet had he done more than sound each note as he made it, trying it, softening it by tender devices with the wood; but now the hour was come when he should gather down the soul of the Golden Pipes to his fingers, and give to the ears of the world the song of the morning stars, the music of Jubal and his comrades, the affluent melody to which the sons of men, in the first days, paced the world in time with the thoughts of God. For days he lived alone in the cedar-house—and who may know what he was doing dreaming, listening, or praying? Then the word went through the valley and the hills that one evening he would play for all who came; and that day was "Toussaint," or the Feast of All Souls.

So they came both old and young, and they did not enter the house, but waited outside, upon the mossy rocks, or sat among the trees, and watched the heavy sun roll down and the Golden Pipes flame in the light of evening. Far beneath in the valley the water ran lightly on, but there came no sound from it, none from anywhere; only a general pervasive murmur quieting to the heart.

Now they heard a note come from the organ—a soft low sound that seemed to rise out of the good earth and mingle with the vibrant air, the song of birds, the whisper of trees, and the murmuring water. Then came another, and another note, then chords, and chords upon these, and by-and-by, rolling tides of melody, until, as it seemed to the listeners, the air ached with the incomparable song; and men and women wept, and children hid their heads in the laps of their mothers, and young men and maidens dreamed dreams never to be forgotten. For one short hour the music went on, then twilight came. Presently the sounds grew fainter, and exquisitely painful, and now a low sob seemed to pass through all the heart of the organ, and then silence fell, and in the sacred pause, Hepnon came out among them all, pale and desolate. He looked at them a minute most sadly, and then lifting up his arms towards the Golden Pipes, now hidden in the dusk, he cried low and brokenly:

"O my God, give me back my dream!"

Then his crutch seemed to give way beneath him, and he sank upon the ground, faint and gasping.

They raised him up, and women and men whispered in his ear

"Ah, the beautiful, beautiful music, Hepnon!" But he only said: "O my God, O my God, give me back my dream!" When he had said it thrice, he turned his face to where his organ was in the cedar-house, and then his eyes closed, and he fell asleep: and they could not wake him. But at sunrise the next morning a shiver passed through him, and then a cold quiet stole over him, and Hepnon and the music of the Golden Pipes departed from the Voshti Hills, and came again no more.

THE GUARDIAN OF THE FIRE

"Height unto height answereth knowledge."

His was the first watch, the farthest fire, for Shaknon Hill towered above the great gulf, and looked back also over thirty leagues of country towards the great city. There came a time again when all the land was threatened. From sovereign lands far off, two fleets were sailing hard to reach the wide basin before the walled city, the one to save, the other to destroy. If Tinoir, the Guardian of the Fire, should sight the destroying fleet, he must light two fires on Shaknon Hill, and then, at the edge of the wide basin, in a treacherous channel, the people would send out fire-rafts to burn the ships of the foe. Five times in the past had Tinoir been the Guardian of the Fire, and five times had the people praised him; but praise and his scanty wage were all he got.

The hut in which he lived with his wife on another hill, ten miles from Shaknon, had but two rooms, and their little farm and the garden gave them only enough to live—no more. Elsewhere there was good land in abundance, but it had been said years ago to Tinoir by the great men, that he should live not far from Shaknon, so that in times of peril he might guard the fire and be sentinel for all the people. Perhaps Tinoir was too dull to see that he was giving all and getting naught; that while he waited and watched he was always poor, and also was getting old. There was no house or home within fifty miles of them, and only now and then some wandering Indians lifted the latch, and drew in beside their hearth, or a good priest with a soul of love for others, came and said Mass in the room where a little Calvary had been put up. Two children had come and gone, and Tinoir and Dalice had dug their graves and put them in a warm nest of maple leaves, and afterwards lived upon the memories of them. But after these two, children came no more; and Tinoir and Dalice grew closer and closer to each other, coming to look alike in face, as they had long been alike in mind and feeling. None ever lived nearer to nature than they, and wild things grew to be their friends; so that you might see Dalice at her door tossing crumbs with one hand to birds, and with the other bits of meat to foxes, martens, and wild dogs, which came and went unharmed by them. Tinoir shot no wild animals for profit—only for food and for skins and furs to wear. Because of this he was laughed at by all who knew, save the priest of St. Sulpice, who, on Easter Day, when the little man came yearly to Mass over two hundred miles of country, praised him to his people, and made much of him, though Tinoir was not vain enough to see it.

When word came down the river, and up over the hills to Tinoir, that war was come and that he must go to watch for the hostile fleet and for the friendly fleet as well, he made no murmur, though it was the time of harvest, and Dalice had had a sickness from which she was not yet recovered.

"Go, my Tinoir," said Dalice, with a little smile, "and I will reap the grain. If your eyes are sharp you shall see my bright sickle moving in the sun."

"There is the churning of the milk too, Dalice," answered Tinoir; "you are not strong, and sometimes the butter comes slow; and there's the milking also."

"Strength is coming to me fast, Tinoir," she said, and drew herself up; but her dress lay almost flat on her bosom. Tinoir took her arm and felt it above the elbow.

"It is like the muscle of a little child," he said.

"But I will drink those bottles of red wine the Governor sent the last time you watched the fire on Shaknon," she said, brightening up, and trying to cheer him. He nodded, for he saw what she was trying to do, and said: "Also a little of the gentian and orange root three times a day-eh, Dalice?"

After arranging for certain signs, by little fires, which they were to light upon the hills and so speak with each other, they said, "Good day, Dalice," and "Good day, Tinoir," drank a glass of the red wine, and added: "Thank the good God;" then Tinoir wiped his mouth with his sleeve, and went away, leaving Dalice with a broken glass at her feet, and a look in her eyes which it was well that Tinoir did not see.

But as he went he was thinking how, the night before, Dalice had lain with her arm round his neck hour after hour as she slept, as she did before they ever had a child; and that even in her sleep, she kissed him as she used to kiss him before he brought her away from the parish of Ste. Genevieve to be his wife. And the more he thought about it the happier he became, and more than once he stopped and shook his head in pleased retrospection. And Dalice thought of it too as she hung over the churn, her face drawn and tired and shining with sweat; and she shook her head, and tears came into her eyes, for she saw further into things than Tinoir. And once as she passed his coat on the wall, she rubbed it softly with her hand, as she might his curly head when he lay beside her.

7

From Shaknon Tinoir watched; but of course he could never see her bright sickle shining, and he could not know whether her dress still hung loose upon her breast, or whether the flesh of her arms was still like a child's. If all was well with Dalice a little fire should be lighted at the house door just at the going down of the sun, and it should be at once put out. If she was ill, a fire should be lit and then put out two hours after sundown. If she should be ill beyond any help, this fire should burn on till it went out.

Day after day Tinoir, as he watched for the coming fleet, saw the fire lit at sundown, and then put out. But one night the fire did not come till two hours after sundown, and it was put out at once. He fretted much, and he prayed that Dalice might be better, and he kept to his post, looking for the fleet of the foe. Evening after evening was this other fire lighted and then put out at once; and a great longing came to him to leave this guarding of the fire, and go to her—"For half a day," he said—"just for half a day!" But in that half day the fleet might pass, and then it would be said that Tinoir had betrayed his country. At last sleep left him, and he fought a demon night and day; and always he remembered Dalice's arm about his neck, and her kisses that last night they were together. Twice he started away from his post to go to her, but before he had gone a hundred paces he came back.

At last one afternoon he saw ships, not far off, rounding the great cape in the gulf, and after a time, at sunset, he knew by their shape it was the fleet of the foe; and so he lighted his great fires, and they were answered leagues away towards the city by another beacon.

Two hours after sunset of this day the fire in front of Tinoir's home was lighted, and was not put out, and Tinoir sat and watched it till it died away. So he lay in the light of his own great war-fire till morning, for he could not travel at night, and then, his duty over, he went back to his home. He found Dalice lying beside the ashes of her fire, past hearing all he said in her ear, unheeding the kiss he set upon her lips.

Two nights afterwards, coming back from laying her beside her children, he saw a great light in the sky towards the city, as of a huge fire. When the courier came to him bearing the Governor's message and the praise of the people, and told of the enemy's fleet destroyed by the fire-rafts, he stared at the man, then turned his head to a place where a pine cross showed against the green grass, and said:

"Dalice—my wife—is dead."

8

"You have saved your country, Tinoir," answered the courier kindly.

"I have lost Dalice!" he said, and fondled the rosary Dalice used to carry when she lived; and he would speak to the man no more.

BY THAT PLACE CALLED PERADVENTURE

By that place called Peradventure in the Voshti Hills dwelt Golgothar the strong man, who, it was said, could break an iron pot with a blow, or pull a tall sapling from the ground.

"If I had a hundred men so strong," said Golgothar, "I would go and conquer Nooni, the city of our foes."

Because he had not the hundred men he did not go; and Nooni still sent insults to the country of Golgothar, and none could travel safe between the capitals. And Golgothar was sorry.

"If I had a hundred men so strong," said Golgothar, "I would build a dyke to keep the floods back from the people crowded on the lowlands."

Because he had not the hundred men, now and again the floods came down, and swept the poor folk out to sea, or laid low their habitations. And Golgothar pitied them.

"If I had a hundred men so strong," said Golgothar, "I would clear the wild boar from the forests that the children should not fear to play among the trees."

Because he had not the hundred men the graves of children multiplied, and countless mothers sat by empty beds and mourned. And Golgothar put his head between his knees in trouble for them.

"If I had a hundred men so strong," said Golgothar, "I would with great stones mend the broken pier, and the bridge between the islands should not fall." Because he had not the hundred men, at last the bridge gave way, and a legion of the king's army were carried to the whirlpool, where they fought in vain. And Golgothar made a feast of remembrance to them, and tears dripped on his beard when he said: "Hail and Farewell!"

"If I had a hundred men so strong," said Golgothar, "I would go against the walls of chains our rebels built, and break them one by one."

Because he had not the hundred men, the chain walls blocked the only pass between the hills, and so cut in two the kingdom: and they who pined for corn went wanting, and they who yearned for fish stayed hungry. And Golgothar, brooding, said his heart bled for his country.

"If I had a hundred men so strong," said Golgothar, "I would go among the thousand brigands of Mirnan, and bring again the beloved daughter of our city."

Because he had not the hundred men the beloved lady languished in her prison, for the brigands asked as ransom the city of Talgone which they hated. And Golgothar carried in his breast a stone image she had given him, and for very grief let no man speak her name before him.

"If I had a hundred men so strong—" said Golgothar, one day, standing on a great point of land and looking down the valley.

As he said it, he heard a laugh, and looking down he saw Sapphire, or Laugh of the Hills, as she was called. A long staff of iron-wood was in her hands, with which she jumped the dykes and streams and rocky fissures; in her breast were yellow roses, and there was a tuft of pretty feathers in her hair. She reached up and touched him on the breast with her staff, then she laughed again, and sang a snatch of song in mockery:

>*"I am a king,*
>
>*I have no crown,*
>
>*I have no throne to sit in—"*

"Pull me up, boy," she said. She wound a leg about the staff, and, taking hold, he drew her up as if she had been a feather.

"If I had a hundred mouths I would kiss you for that," she said, still mocking; "but having only one, I'll give it to the cat, and weep for Golgothar."

"Silly jade," he said, and turned towards his tent.

As they passed a slippery and dangerous place, where was one strong solitary tree, she suddenly threw a noose over him, drew it fast and sprang far out over the precipice into the air. Even as she did so, he jumped behind the tree, and clasped it, else on the slippery place he would have gone over with her. The rope came taut, and presently he drew her up again to safety, and while she laughed at him and mocked him, he held her tight under his arm, and carried her to his lodge, where he let her go.

"Why did you do it, devil's madcap?" he asked.

11

"Why didn't you wait for the hundred men so strong?" she laughed.

"Why did you jump behind the tree?

"'If I had a hundred men, height,

I would buy my corn for a penny a gill.

If I had a hundred men or so,

I would dig a grave for the maid of the hill, height!'"

He did not answer her, but stirred the soup in the pot and tasted it, and hung a great piece of meat over the fire. Then he sat down, and only once did he show anger as she mocked him, and that was when she thrust her hand into his breast, took out the little stone image, and said:

"If a little stone god had a hundred hearts,

Would a little stone goddess trust in one?"

Then she made as if she would throw it into the fire, but he caught her hand and crushed it, so that she cried out for pain and anger, and said:

"Brute of iron, go break the posts in the brigands' prison-house, but leave a poor girl's wrist alone. If I had a hundred men—" she added, mocking wildly again, and then, springing at him, put her two thumbs at the corners of his eyes, and cried: "Stir a hand, and out they will come—your eyes for my bones!"

He did not stir till her fury was gone. Then he made her sit down and eat with him, and afterwards she said softly to him, and without a laugh: "Why should the people say, 'Golgothar is our shame, for he has great strength, and yet he does nothing but throw great stones for sport into the sea'?"

He had the simple mind of a child, and he listened to her patiently, and at last got up and began preparing for a journey, cleaning all his weapons, and gathering them together. She understood him, and she said, with a little laugh like music: "One strong man is better than a hundred—a little key will open a great door easier than a hundred hammers. What is the strength of a hundred bullocks without this?" she added, tapping him on the forehead.

Then they sat down and talked together quietly for a long time; and at sunset she saw him start away upon great errands.

Before two years had gone, Nuoni, the city of their foes, was taken; the chain wall of the rebels opened to the fish and corn of the poor; the children wandered in the forest without fear of wild boars; the dyke was built to save the people in the lowlands; and Golgothar carried to the castle the King had given him the daughter of the city, freed from Mirnan.

"If Golgothar had a hundred wives—" said a voice to the strong man as he entered the castle gates. Looking up he saw Sapphire. He stretched out his hand to her in joy and friendship.

"—I would not be one of them," she added, with a mocking laugh, as she dropped from the wall, leaped the moat by the help of her staff, and danced away laughing. There are those who say, however that tears fell down her cheeks as she laughed.

THE SINGING OF THE BEES

"Mother, didst thou not say thy prayers last night?"

"Twice, my child."

"Once before the little shrine, and once beside my bed—is it not so?"

"It is so, my Fanchon. What hast thou in thy mind?"

"Thou didst pray that the storm die in the hills, and the flood cease, and that my father come before it was again the hour of prayer. It is now the hour. Canst thou not hear the storm and the wash of the flood? And my father does not come!"

"Dear Fanchon, God is good."

"When thou wast asleep I rose from my bed, and in the dark I kissed the feet of—Him—on the little Calvary; and I did not speak, but in my heart I called."

"What didst thou call, my child?"

"I called to my father: 'Come back-come back!'"

"Thou shouldst have called to God, my Fanchon."

"I loved my father, and I called to him."

"Thou shouldst love God."

"I knew my father first. If God loved thee, He would answer thy prayer. Dost thou not hear the cracking of the cedar trees and the cry of the wolves—they are afraid. All day and all night the rain and wind come down, and the birds and wild fowl have no peace. I kissed—His feet, and my throat was full of tears; but I called in my heart. Yet the storm and the dark stay, and my father does not come."

"Let us be patient, my Fanchon."

"He went to guide the priest across the hills. Why does not God guide him back?"

"My Fanchon, let us be patient."

14

"The priest was young, and my father has grey hair."

"Wilt thou not be patient, my child?"

"He filled the knapsack of the priest with food better than his own, and—thou didst not see it—put money in his hand."

"My own, the storm may pass."

"He told the priest to think upon our home as a little nest God set up here for such as he."

"There are places of shelter in the hills for thy father, my Fanchon."

"And when the priest prayed, 'That Thou mayst bring us safely to this place where we would go,' my father said so softly, 'We beseech Thee to hear us, good Lord!'"

"My Fanchon, thy father hath gone this trail many times."

"The prayer was for the out-trail, not the in-trail, my mother."

"Nay, I do not understand thee."

"A swarm of bees came singing through the room last night, my mother. It was dark and I could not see, but there was a sweet smell, and I heard the voices."

"My child, thou art tired with watching, and thy mind is full of fancies. Thou must sleep."

"I am tired of watching. Through the singing of the bees as they passed over my bed, I heard my father's voice. I could not hear the words, they seemed so far away, like the voices of the bees; and I did not cry out, for the tears were in my throat. After a moment the room was so still that it made my heart ache."

"Oh, my Fanchon, my child, thou dost break my heart! Dost thou not know the holy words?"

"'And their souls do pass like singing bees, where no man may follow. These are they whom God gathereth out of the whirlwind and the desert, and bringeth home in a goodly swarm.'"

Night drew close to the earth, and as suddenly as a sluice-gate drops and holds back a flood the storm ceased. Along the crest of the hills there slowly grew a line of light, and then the serene moon came up and on, persistent to give the earth love where it had had punishment. Divers flocks of clouds, camp-followers of the storm, could not abash her. But once she drew shrinking back behind a slow troup of them; for down at the bottom of a gorge lay a mountaineer, face upward and unmoving, as he had lain since a rock loosened beneath him, and the depths swallowed him. If he had had ears to hear, he would have answered the soft, bitter cries which rose from a but on the Voshti Hills above him:

"Michel, Michel, art thou gone?"

"Come back, oh, my father, come back!"

But perhaps it did avail that there were lighted candles before a little shrine, and that a mother, in her darkness, kissed the feet of One on a Calvary.

THE WHITE OMEN

"Ah, Monsieur, Monsieur, come quick!"

"My son, wilt thou not be patient?"

"But she—my Fanchon—and the child!"

"I knew thy Fanchon, and her father, when thou wast yet a child."

"But they may die before we come, Monsieur."

"These things are in God's hands, Gustave."

"You are not a father; you have never known what makes the world seem nothing."

"I knew thy Fanchon's father."

"Is that the same?"

"There are those who save and those who die for others. Of thy love thou wouldst save—the woman hath lain in thine arms, the child is of this. But to thy Fanchon's father I was merely a priest—we had not hunted together nor met often about the fire, and drew fast the curtains for the tales which bring men close. He took me safely on the out-trail, but on the home-trail he was cast away. Dost thou not think the love of him that stays as great as the love of him that goes?"

"Ah, thou wouldst go far to serve my wife and child!"

"Love knows not distance; it hath no continent; its eyes are for the stars, its feet for the swords; it continueth, though an army lay waste the pasture; it comforteth when there are no medicines; it hath the relish of manna; and by it do men live in the desert."

"But if it pass from a man, that which he loves, and he is left alone, Monsieur?"

"That which is loved may pass, but love hath no end."

"Thou didst love my Fanchon's father?"

"I prayed him not to go, for a storm was on, but there was the thought of wife and child on him—the good Michel—and he said: 'It is the home-trail, and I must get to my nest.' Poor soul, poor soul! I who carry my life as a leaf in autumn for the west wind was saved, and he—!"

"We are on the same trail now, Monsieur?"

"See: how soft a night, and how goodly is the moon!"

"It is the same trail now as then, Monsieur?"

"And how like velvet are the shadows in the gorge there below—like velvet-velvet."

"Like a pall. He travelled this trail, Monsieur?"

"I remember thy Fanchon that night—so small a child was she, with deep brown eyes, a cloud of hair that waved about her head, and a face that shone like spring. I have seen her but once since then, and yet thou sayest thy Fanchon has now her great hour, that she brings forth?"

"Yes. In the morning she cried out to me twice, for I am not easy of waking—shame to me—and said: 'Gustave, thou shalt go for the priest over the hills, for my time is at hand, and I have seen the White Omen on the wall.' The White Omen—you know, Monsieur?"

"What does such as she with the legend of the White Omen, Gustave?"

"Who can tell what is in the heart of a mother? Their eyes are not the eyes of such as we."

"Neither the eyes of man nor priest—thou sayest well. How did she see it?"

"She was lying in a soft sleep, when something like a pain struck through her eyes, and she waked. There upon the wall over the shrine was the white arrow with the tuft of fire. It came and went three times, and then she called me."

"What tale told the arrow to thy Fanchon, Gustave?"

"That for the child which cometh into the world a life must go from the world."

"The world is wide and souls are many, Gustave."

"Most true; but her heart was heavy, and it came upon her that the child might be spared and herself taken."

"Is not that the light of thy home—yonder against the bunch of firs?"

"Yes, yes, good father, they have put a light in the window. See, see, there are two lights. Ah, merci, merci, they both live! She hath had her hour! That was the sign our mother promised me."

"Michel's wife—ah, yes, Michel's wife! Blessed be God. A moment, Gustave; let us kneel here..."

... "Monsieur, did you not see a white arrow shoot down the sky as the prayer ended?"

"My son, it was a falling star."

"It seemed to have a tuft of fire."

"Hast thou also the mind of a woman, Gustave?"

"I cannot tell. If it was not a human soul it was a world, and death is death."

"Thou shalt think of life, Gustave. In thy nest there are two birds where was but one. Keep in thy heart the joy of life and the truth of love, and the White Omen shall be naught to thee."

"May I say 'thou' as I speak?"

"Thou shalt speak as I speak to thee."

"Thy face is pale-art thou ill, mon pere?"

"I have no beard, and the moon shines in my face."

"Thy look is as that of one without sight."

"Nay, nay, I can see the two lights in thy window, my son."

"Joy—joy, a little while, and I shall clasp my Fanchon in my arms!"

"Thy Fanchon, and the child—and the child."

The fire sent a trembling glow through the room of a hut on a Voshti hill, and the smell of burning fir and camphire wood filtered through the air with a sleepy sweetness. So delicate and faint between the quilts lay the young mother, the little Fanchon, a shining wonder still in her face, and the exquisite touch of birth on her—for when a child is born the mother also is born again. So still she lay until one who gave her into the world stooped, and drawing open the linen at her breast, nestled a little life there, which presently gave a tiny cry, the first since it came forth. Then Fanchon's arms drew up, and, with eyes all tenderly burning, she clasped the babe to her breast, and as silk breast touched silk cheek, there sprang up in her the delight and knowledge that the doom of the White Omen was not for herself. Then she called the child by its father's name, and said into the distance: "Gustave, Gustave, come back!"

And the mother of Fanchon, remembering one night so many years before, said, under her breath: "Michel, Michel, thou art gone so long!"

With their speaking, Gustave and the priest entered on them; and Fanchon crying out for joy, said:

"Kiss thy child—thy little Gustave, my husband." Then, to the priest:

"Last night I saw the White Omen, mon pere; and one could not die, nor let the child die, without a blessing. But we shall both live now."
The priest blessed all, and long time he talked with the wife of the lost Michel. When he rose to go to bed she said to him: "The journey has been too long, mon pere. Your face is pale and you tremble. Youth has no patience. Gustave hurried you."
"Gustave yearned for thy Fanchon and the child. The White Omen made him afraid."
"But the journey was too much. It is a hard, a bitter trail."
"I have come gladly as I went once with thy Michel. But, as thou sayest, I am tired—at my heart. I will get to my rest."
Near dawn Gustave started from the bed where he sat watching, for he saw the White Omen over against the shrine, and then a voice said, as it were out of a great distance:
"Even me also, O my father!"

With awed footsteps, going to see, he found that a man had passed out upon that trail by which no hunter from life can set a mark to guide a comrade; leaving behind the bones and flesh which God set up, too heavy to carry on so long a journey.

THE SOJOURNERS

"My father, shall we soon be there?"

The man stopped, and shading his eyes with his hand, looked long before him into the silver haze. They were on the southern bank of a wide valley, flanked by deep hills looking wise as grey-headed youth, a legion of close comrades, showing no gap in their ranks. They seemed to breathe; to sit, looking down into the valley, with heads dropped on their breasts, and deep overshadowed eyes, that never changed, in mist or snow, or sun, or any kind of weather: dark brooding lights that knew the secrets of the world, watchful yet kind. Races, ardent with longing, had come and gone through the valley, had passed the shining porches in the North on the way to the quiet country; and they had never come again, though shadows flitted back and forth when the mists came down: visiting spirits, hungering on the old trail for some that had dropped by the way. As the ages passed, fewer and fewer travelled through the valley-no longer a people or a race, but twos and threes, and sometimes a small company, like soldiers of a battered guard, and oftener still solitary pilgrims, broken with much travel and bowed with loneliness. But they always cried out with joy when they beheld far off in the North, at the end of the long trail, this range of grey and violet hills break into golden gaps with scarlet walls, and rivers of water ride through them pleasantly. Then they hurried on to the opal haze that hung at the end of the valley—and who heard ever of any that wished to leave the Scarlet Hills and the quiet country beyond!

The boy repeated his question: "My father, shall we soon be there?"

The man withdrew his hand from over his eyes, and a strange smile came to his lips.

"My son," he answered, "canst thou not see? Yonder, through the gentle mist, are the Scarlet Hills. Our journey is near done."

The boy lifted his head and looked. "I can see nothing but the mist, my father—not the Scarlet Hills. I am tired, I would sleep."

"Thou shalt sleep soon. The wise men told us of the Delightful Chateau at the gateway of the hills. Courage, my son! If I gave thee the golden balls to toss, would it cheer thee?"

"My father, I care not for the golden balls; but if I had horse and sword and a thousand men, I would take a city."

The man laid his hand upon the boy's shoulder.

"If I, my son," he said, "had a horse and sword and a thousand men, I would build a city."

"Why dost thou not fly thy falcon, or write thy thoughts upon the sand, as thou didst yesterday, my father?"

The man loosed the falcon from his wrist, and watched it fly away.

"My son, I care not for the falcon, nor any more for writing on the sands."

"My father, if thou didst build a city, I would not tear it down, but I would keep it with my thousand men.

"Thou hast well said, my son." And the man stooped and kissed the lad on the forehead.

And so they travelled on in silence for a long time, and slowly they came to the opal haze, which smelled sweet as floating flowers, and gave their hearts a halcyon restfulness. And glancing down at him many times, the father saw the lad's face look serenely wise, without becoming old, and his brown hair clustered on his forehead with all the life of youth in it. Yet in his eyes the lad seemed as old as himself.

"My father," said the lad again, "wouldst thou then build a city?"

And the father answered: "Nay, my son, I would sow seed, and gather it into harvest—enough for my needs, no more; and sit quiet in my doorway when my work was done, and be grateful to the gods."

The lad waited a moment, then answered: "When thou wast a governor in our own country, thou hadst serfs and retainers without number, and fifty men to beat upon the shields of brass to tell of thy coming through the gates of the King's house; now thou wouldst sow a field and sit quiet in thy doorway, like the blind seller of seed-cakes 'gainst the temple."

"Even so, my son." Then he stooped down, knelt upon his knees, and kissed the earth solemnly, and when he rose there was a smile upon his face.

Then the lad said: "When I was the son of a governor I loved to play with the golden balls, to shoot at the target for pearls, and to ride the flamingo down; now I would grind the corn which thou didst reap, and with oil make seed-cakes for our supper, and sit quiet with thee in thy doorway." Then he too stooped down and kissed the earth, and rose up again with a smile upon his face.

And as they went the earth seemed suddenly to blossom anew, the glory of the Scarlet Hills burst upon them, and they could hear bugles calling far off and see giant figures trooping along the hills, all scarlet too, with streaming hair. And presently, near to a lake, there was a great gateway, and perched upon a rock near it a chateau of divine proportions, on which was written above the perfect doorway:

"The Keeper of the House awaits thee. Enter into Quiet."

And they entered, and were possessed of an incomparable peace. And then came to them an old man of noble countenance, with eye neither dimmed nor sunken, and cheek dewy as a child's, and his voice was like an organ when it plays the soft thanksgiving of a mother.

"Why did ye kiss the earth as ye travelled?" he asked. Then they told him, each with his own tongue, and he smiled upon them and questioned them of all their speech by the way; and they answered him all honestly and with gladness, for the searching of their hearts was a joy and relief. But he looked most lovingly upon the lad.

"Wouldst thou, then, indeed enter the quiet country?" he asked.

And the lad answered: "I have lived so long in the noise!"

"Thou hast learned all, thou hast lived all," he answered the boy. "Beyond the Hills of Scarlet there is quiet, and thou shalt dwell there, thou and he. Ye have the perfect desire—Go in peace, and know that though ye are of different years, as men count time, God's clock strikes the same for both; for both are of equal knowledge, and have the same desire at last."

Then, lifting up his hands, he said: "O children of men! O noisy world! when will ye learn the delectable way?"

Slowly they all three came from the Chateau, and through the great gateway, and passed to the margin of a shining lake. There the two stepped into a boat that waited for them, of which the rowers were nobly fashioned, like the Keeper of the House, and as they bowed their heads to a melodious blessing, the boat drew away. Soon, in the sweet haze, they looked transfigured and enlarged, majestic figures moving through the Scarlet Hills to the quiet country. Now the valley through which they had passed was the Valley of Death, where the young become old, and the old young, and all become wise.

THE TENT OF THE PURPLE MAT

The Tent stands on the Mount of Lost Winters, in that bit of hospitable land called the Fair Valley, which is like no other in the North. Whence comes the soft wind that comforts it, who can tell? It swims through the great gap in the mountains, and passing down the valley, sinks upon the prairie of the Ten Stars, where it is lost. What man first placed the Tent on the Mount none knows, though legends are many. It has a clear outlook to the north, whence comes the gracious wind, and it is sheltered at the south by a stout wall of commendable trees; yet these are at some small distance, so that the Tent has a space all about it, and the figure of the general land is as that of an amphitheatre.

It is made of deerskin, dyed by a strange process which turned it white, and doctored by some cunning medicine. It is like a perfect parchment, and shows no decay. It has a centre-pole of excellent fir, and from its peak flies a strip of snake-skin, dyed a red which never fades. For the greater part of the year the plateau whereon the Tent stands is covered with a sweet grass, and when the grass dies there comes a fine white frost, ungoverned by the sun, in which the footstep sinks, as into an unfilled honeycomb.

The land has few clouds, and no storms, save of the lightest-rain which is as mist, and snow which is as frosty haze. The sun cherishes the place continually, and the moon rises on it with a large rejoicing.

Yet no man dwells in the valley. It is many scores of leagues from any habitation, from the lodges of the Indians or the posts of the Company's people. There are few tribes that know of it, and these go not to it as tribes, but as one man or one woman has need. Men say that beyond it, in another amphitheatre of the hills, is the White Valley, the Place of Peace, where the sleepers are, and the Scarlet Hunter is sentinel. Yet who knows—since any that have been there are constrained to be silent, or forget what they have seen?

But this valley where the Tent stands is for those who have broken the commandment, "Thou shalt not sell thy soul." Hither they come and wait and desire continually; and this delightful land is their punishment, for they have no relish for goodly things, the power to enjoy going from them when they bargained their souls away. The great peace, the noble pasturage, the equal joy of day and night wherein is neither heat nor cold, where life is like the haze on a harvest-field, are for chastisement, till that by great patience and striving, some one, having the gift of sacrifice, shall give his life to buy back that soul.

For it is in the minds of this people of the North that for every life that comes into the world one passes out, and for every soul which is bartered away another must be set free ere it can be redeemed.

Men and women whom life and their own sins had battered came seeking the Tent; but they were few and they were chiefly old, for conscience cometh mostly when man can work and wanton no more. Yet one day, when the sight of the valley was most fair to their eyes, there came out of the southmost corner a girl, who, as soon as she set foot in the valley, laid aside her knapsack in the hollow of a tree, also her moccasins and a little cap of fur, and came on with bare head and feet towards the Mount of the Lost Winters.

She was of good stature, ripely made, not beautiful of face, but with a look which would make any man turn twice to see, a very glory of fine hair, and a hand which spoke oftener than the lips. She had come a month's travel, scarcely halting from sunrise to sunset, and she was as worn in body as in spirit. Now, as she passed up the valley she stood still several times, and looked round in a kind of dream, as well one might who had come out of an inclement south country to this sweet nourishment. Yet she stood not still for joy and content, but for pain. Once or twice she lifted up her hands above her head as though appealing, but these pauses were only for brief moments, for she kept moving on towards the mountain with a swift step. When she had climbed the plateau where the delicate grass yielded with a tender spring to the feet, she paused long and gazed round, as though to take a last glance at all; then, turning to the Tent, looked steadfastly at it, awe and wonder, and something more difficult of interpretation, in her face. At last she slowly came to the curtain of the Tent, and lifting it, without a pause stepped inside, the curtain falling behind her.

The Tent was empty save for the centre-pole, a wooden trough of dried fruit, a jar of water, and a mat of the most gentle purple colour, which was laid between the centre-pole and the tent-curtain. The mat was of exquisite make, as it seemed from the chosen fibres of some perfect wood, and the hue was as that of a Tyrian dye. A soft light pervaded the place, perhaps filtered through the parchment-like white skin of the Tent, for it seemed to have no other fountain. Upon the farther side a token was drawn in purple on the tentskin, and the girl, seeing it, turned quickly to the curtain through which she had passed. Upon the curtain were other signs. She read them slowly, and repeated them out loud in a low uncertain voice, like a bird's note blundering in a flute:

"Four hours shalt thou look northward, kneeling on the Mat of Purple, and thinking of the Camp of the Delightful Fires, around which is the Joyous City; four hours shalt thou lie prone, thy face upon the soothing earth, desiring sleep; and four hours shalt thou look within thine own breast, thinking of thy sin; four hours also shalt thou go through the valley, calling out that thou art lost, and praying the Scarlet Hunter to bring thee home. Afterwards thou shalt sleep, and thou shalt comfort thyself with food when thou wilt. If the Scarlet Hunter comes not, and thy life faileth for misery, and none comprehending thy state offereth his life, that thy soul may be free once more—then thou shalt gladly die, and, yielding thine own body, shall purchase back thy soul; but this is not possible until thou hast dwelt here a year and a day."

Having read, the girl threw herself face forward on the ground, her body shaking with grief, and she cried out a man's name many times with great bitterness "Ambroise! Ambroise! Ambroise!"

A long time she lay prone, crying so; but at last arose and, folding back the curtain with hot hands, began her vigil for the redemption of a soul.

And while her sorrow grew, a father mourned for his daughter and called his God to witness that he was guiltless of her loss, though he had said hard words to her by reason of a man called Ambroise. Then, too, the preacher had exhorted her late and early till her mind was in a maze—it is enough to have the pangs of youth and love, to be awakened by the pain of mere growth and knowledge, without the counsel of the overwise to go jolting through the soul.

The girl was only eighteen. She had never known her mother, she had lived as the flowers do, and when her hour of trial came she felt herself cast like a wandering bird out of the nest. In her childhood she had known no preachers, no teaching, save the wholesome catechism of a father's love and the sacred intimacy of Nature. Living so, learning by signs the language of law and wisdom, she had indrawn the significance of legend, the power of the awful natural. She had made her own commandments.

When Ambroise the courier came, she had looked into his eyes and seen her own—indeed, it was most wonderful, for those two pairs of eyes were as those of one person. And each, as each looked, smiled—that smile which is the coming laughter of a heart at itself. Yet they were different—he a man, she a woman; he versed in evil, she taught in good; he a vagrant of the snows, the fruit of whose life was like the contemptible stones of the desert; she the keeper of a goodly lodge, past which flowed a water that went softly, making rich the land, the fountain of her perfect deeds. He, looking into her eyes, saw himself when he had no sin on his soul; and she into his—as it seemed, her own always—saw herself as it were in a cobweb of evils which she could not understand. As his heart grew lighter, hers grew sick, even when she knew that these were the only eyes in which she could ever see happiness.

It grew upon her that Ambroise's sins were hers and not his; that she, not he, had bartered a soul for the wages of sin. When they said at the Fort that her eyes and Ambroise's, and her face and his, were as of one piece, the pain of the thought deepened, and other pains came likewise, for her father and the preacher urged that a man who had sold himself to the devil was no comrade for her in little or much. Yet she loved him as only they can who love for the first time, and with the deep primitive emotions which are out of the core of nature. But her heart had been cloven as by a wedge, and she would not, and could not, lie in his arms, nor rest her cheek to his, nor seek that haven where true love is fastened like a nail on the wall of that inn called home. He was herself, he must be brought back; and so, one night, while yet the winter was on, she stole away out of the Fort, pausing at his door a moment only, laying her hand upon it as one might tenderly lay it on the brow of a sick sleeper. Then she stepped away out on the plains, pointing her course by the moon, for the Mount of Lost Winters and the Tent of the Purple Mat.

When the people of the Fort waked, and it was found that she was gone, search parties sallied out, but returned as they went after many days. And at last, because Ambroise suffered as one ground between rolling stones, even the preacher and the father of the girl relented towards him. After some weeks there came word through a wandering tribe that the body of a girl had been found on the Child o' Sin River, and black pelts were hung as mourning on the lodges and houses and walls of the Fort, and the father shut himself in his room, admitting no one. Still, they mourned without great cause.

But, if the girl had taken the sins of Ambroise with her, she had left him beside that soft flowing river of her goodness; and the savour of the herbs on its banks was to him like the sun on a patch of pennyroyal, bringing medicine to the sick body through the nostrils. So one morning, after many months, having crept from the covert of remorse, he took a guide to start him in the right trail, and began his journey to the Valley, whither she had gone before him, though he knew it not. From the moment that his guide left him dangers beset him, and those spirits called the Mockers, which are the evil deeds of a man crying to Heaven, came crying about him from the dead white trees, breathing through the powdery air, whistling down the moonlight; so that to cheer him he called out again and again, like any heathen:

"Keeper, O Keeper of the Kimash Hills!
I am as a dog in the North Sea,
I am as a bat in a cave,
As a lizard am I on a prison wall,
As a tent with no pole,
As a bird with one wing;
I am as a seal in the desert,
I am as a wild horse alone.
O Scarlet Hunter of the Kimash Hills!
Thou hast an arm like a shooting star,
Thou hast an eye like the North Sky fires,
Thou hast a pouch for the hungry,
Thou hast a tent for the lost:
Hear me, O Keeper of the Kimash Hills!"

And whether or not this availed him, who can tell? There be many names of the One Thing, and the human soul hath the same north and south, if there be any north and south and east and west, save in the words of men. But something availed; and one day a footworn traveller, entering the Valley at the southmost corner, laid his cap and bag, moccasins, bow and arrow, and an iron weapon away in a hollow log, seeing not that there were also another bag and cap, and a pair of moccasins there. Then, barefooted and bareheaded, he marched slowly up the Valley, and all its loveliness smote him as a red iron is buffeted at the forge; and an exquisite agony coursed through his veins, so that he cried out, hiding his face. And yet he needs must look and look, all his sight aching with this perfection, never overpowering him, but keeping him ever in the relish of his torture.

At last he came to the door of the Tent in the late evening, and, intent not only to buy back the soul he had marketed—for the sake of the memory of the woman, and believing that none would die for him and that he must die for himself—he lifted the curtain and entered. Then he gave a great cry, for there she lay asleep, face downward, her forehead on the Purple Mat.

"Sherah! Sherah!" he cried, dropping on his knees beside her and lifting up her head.

"Ambroise!" she called out faintly, her pale face drawing away from his breast.

"Sherah, why didst thou come here?" he said. "Thou! thou!"

"To buy back my soul, Ambroise. And this is the last day of the year that I have spent here. Oh, why, why didst thou come? To-morrow all should have been well!"

"To buy back thy soul—thou didst no wrong!" But at that moment their eyes drew close, and changed, and he understood.

"For me—for me!" he whispered.

"Nay, for me!" she replied.

Then they noticed that the Purple Mat on which they knelt was red under their knees, and a goodly light shone through the Tent, not of the day or night. And as they looked amazed, the curtain of the Tent drew open, and one entered, clothed in red from head to foot; and they knew him to be the Scarlet Hunter, the lover of the lost, the Keeper of the Kimash Hills.

Looking at them steadfastly he said to Sherah: "Thou has prevailed. To-night, at the setting of the sun, an old man died in Syria who uttered thy name as in a dream when he passed. The soul of Ambroise hath been bought back by thee."

Then he spoke to Ambroise. "Because thy spirit was willing, and for the woman's sake thou shalt have peace; but this year which she has spent for thee shall be taken from thy life, and added to hers. Come, and I will start ye on the swift trail to your own country, and ye shall come here no more."

As they rose, obeying him, they saw that the red of the Mat had gone a perfect white, and they knew not what to think, for they had acted after the manner of the heathen; but that night, as they travelled with joy towards that Inn called Home, down at the Fort, a preacher with rude noise cried to those who would hear him: "Though your sins be as scarlet they shall become whiter than snow."

THERE WAS A LITTLE CITY

It lay between the mountains and the sea, and a river ran down past it, carrying its good and ill news to a pacific shore, and out upon soft winds, travelling lazily to the scarlet east. All white and a tempered red, it nestled in a valley with other valleys on lower steppes, which seemed as if built by the gods, that they might travel easily from the white-topped mountains, Margath, Shaknon, and the rest, to wash their feet in the sea. In the summer a hot but gracious mistiness softened the green of the valleys, the varying colours of the hills, the blue of the river, the sharp outlines of the cliffs. Along the high shelf of the mountain, muletrains travelled like a procession seen in dreams—slow, hazy, graven yet moving, a part of the ancient hills themselves; upon the river great rafts, manned by scarlet-vested crews, swerved and swam, guided by the gigantic oars which needed five men to lift and swayargonauts they from the sweet-smelling forests to the salt-smelling main. In winter the little city lay still under a coverlet of pure white, with the mists from the river and the great falls above frozen upon the trees, clothing them as graciously as with white samite; so that far as eye could see there was a heavenly purity upon all, covering every mean and distorted thing. There were days when no wind stirred anywhere, and the gorgeous sun made the little city and all the land round about a pretty silver kingdom, where Oberon and his courtiers might have danced and been glad. Often, too, you could hear a distant wood-cutter's axe make a pleasant song in the air, and the wood-cutter himself, as the hickory and steel swung in a shining half-circle to the bole of balsam, was clad in the bright livery of frost, his breath issuing in grey smoke like life itself, mystic and peculiar, man, axe, tree, and breath one common being. And when, by-and-by, the woodcutter added a song of his own to the song his axe made, the illusion was not lost, but rather heightened; for it, too, was part of the unassuming pride of nature, childlike in its simplicity, primeval in its suggestion and expression. The song had a soft monotony, swinging backwards and forwards to the waving axe like the pendulum of a clock. It began with a low humming, as one could think man made before he heard the Voice which taught him how to speak. And then came the words:

> *"None shall stand in the way of the lord,*
> *The lord of the Earth—of the rivers and trees,*
> *Of the cattle and fields and vines!*
> *Hew!*
> *Here shall I build me my cedar home,*
> *A city with gates, a road to the sea*
> *For I am the lord of the Earth!*

Hew! Hew!
Hew and hew, and the sap of the tree
Shall be yours, and your bones shall be strong,
Shall be yours, and your heart shall rejoice,
Shall be yours, and the city be yours,
And the key of its gates be the key
Of the home where your little ones dwell.
Hew and be strong! Hew and rejoice!
For man is the lord of the Earth,
And God is the Lord over all!"

And so long as the little city stands will this same wood-cutter's name and history stand also. He had camped where it stood now, when nothing was there save the wild duck in the reeds, the antelopes upon the hills, and all manner of furred and feathered things; and it all was his. He had seen the yellow flashes of gold in the stream called Pipi, and he had not gathered it, for his life was simple, and he was young enough to cherish in his heart the love of the open world, beyond the desire of cities and the stir of the market-place. In those days there was not a line in his face, not an angle in his body—all smoothly rounded and lithe and alert, like him that was called "the young lion of Dedan." Day by day he drank in the wisdom of the hills and the valleys, and he wrote upon the dried barks of trees the thoughts that came as he lay upon the bearskin in his tent, or cooled his hands and feet, of a hot summer day, in the moist sandy earth, and watched the master of the deer lead his cohorts down the passes of the hills.

But by-and-by mule-trains began to crawl along the ledges of Margath Mountain, and over Shaknon came adventurers, and after them, wandering men seeking a new home, women and children coming also. But when these came he had passed the spring-time of his years, and had grown fixed in the love of the valley, where his sole visitors had been passing tribes of Indians, who knew his moods and trespassed not at all on his domain. The adventurers hungered for the gold in the rivers, and they made it one long washing-trough, where the disease that afflicted them passed on from man to man like poison down a sewer. Then the little city grew, and with the search for gold came other seekings and findings and toilings, and men who came as one stops at an inn to feed, stayed to make their home, and women made the valley cheerful, and children were born, and the pride of the place was as great as that of some village of the crimson East, where every man has ancestors to Mahomet and beyond.

And he, Felion, who had been lord and master of the valley, worked with them, but did not seek for riches, and more often drew away into the hills to find some newer place unspoiled by man. But again and again he returned; for no fire is like the old fire, and no trail like the old trail. And at last it seemed as if he had driven his tent-peg in the Long Valley for ever; for, from among the women who came, he chose one comely and wise and kind, and for five years the world grew older, and Felion did not know it. When he danced his little daughter on his knee, he felt that he had found a new world.

But? a day came when trouble fell upon the little city, for of a sudden the reef of gold was lost, and the great crushing-mills stood idle, and the sound of the hammers was stayed. And they came to Felion, because in his youth he had been of the best of the schoolmen; and he got up from his misery—only the day before his wife had taken a great and lonely journey to that Country which welcomes, but never yields again—and leaving his little child behind, he went down to the mines. And in three days they found the reef once more; for it had curved like the hook of a sickle, and the first arc of the yellow circle had dropped down into the bowels of the earth.

And so he saved the little city from disaster, and the people blessed him at the moment; and the years went on.

Then there came a time when the little city was threatened with a woeful flood, because of a breaking flume; but by a simple and wise device Felion stayed the danger.

And again the people blessed him; and the years went on.

By-and-by an awful peril came, for two-score children had set a great raft loose upon the river, and they drifted down towards the rapids in the sight of the people; and mothers and helpless fathers wrung their hands, for on the swift tide no boat could reach them, and none could intercept the raft. But Felion, seeing, ran out upon the girders of a bridge that was being builded, and there, before them all, as the raft passed under, he let himself fall, breaking his leg as he dropped among the timbers of the fore-part of the raft; for the children were all gathered at the back, where the great oars lay motionless, one dragging in the water behind. Felion drew himself over to the huge oar, and with the strength of five men, while the people watched and prayed, he kept the raft straight for the great slide, else it had gone over the dam and been lost, and all that were thereon. A mile below, the raft was brought to shore, and again the people said that Felion had saved the little city from disaster.

33

And they blessed him for the moment; and the years went on.

Felion's daughter grew towards womanhood, and her beauty was great, and she was welcome everywhere in the valley, the people speaking well of her for her own sake. But at last a time came when of the men of the valley one called, and Felion's daughter came quickly to him, and with tears for her father and smiles for her husband, she left the valley and journeyed into the east, having sworn to love and cherish him while she lived. And her father, left solitary, mourned for her, and drew away into a hill above the valley in a cedar house that he built; and having little else to love, loved the earth, and sky, and animals, and the children from the little city when they came his way. But his heart was sore; for by-and-by no letters came from his daughter, and the little city, having prospered, concerned it self no more with him. When he came into its streets there were those who laughed, for he was very tall and rude, and his grey hair hung loose on his shoulders, and his dress was still a hunter's. They had not long remembered the time when a grievous disease, like a plague, fell upon the place, and people died by scores, as sheep fall in a murrain. And again they had turned to him, and he, because he knew of a miraculous medicine got from Indian sachems, whose people had suffered of this sickness, came into the little city, and by his medicines and fearless love and kindness stayed the plague.

And thus once more he saved the little city from disaster, and they blessed him for the moment; and the years went on.

In time they ceased to think of Felion at all, and he was left alone; even the children came no more to visit him; and he had pleasure only in hunting and shooting and in felling trees, with which he built a high stockade and a fine cedar house within it. And all the work of this he did with his own hands, even to the polishing of the floors and the carved work of the large fireplaces. Yet he never lived in the house, nor in any room of it, and the stockade gate was always shut; and when any people passed that way they stared and shrugged their shoulders, and thought Felion mad or a fool. But he was wise in his own way, which was not the way of those who had reason to bless him for ever, and who forgot him, though he had served them through so many years. Against the little city he had an exceeding bitterness; and this grew, and had it not been that his heart was kept young by the love of the earth, and the beasts about him in the hills, he must needs have cursed the place and died. But the sight of a bird in the nest with her young, and the smell of a lair, and the light of the dawn that came out of the east, and the winds that came up from the sea, and the hope that would not die kept him from being of those who love not life for life's sake, be it in ease or in sorrow. He was of those who find all worth the doing, even all worth the suffering; and so, though he frowned and his lips drew tight with anger when he looked down at the little city, he felt that elsewhere in the world there was that which made it worth the saving.

If his daughter had been with him he would have laughed at that which his own hands had founded, protected, and saved. But no word came from her, and laughter was never on his lips—only an occasional smile when, perhaps, he saw two sparrows fighting, or watched the fish chase each other in the river, or a toad, too lazy to jump, walk stupidly like a convict, dragging his long, green legs behind him. And when Felion looked up towards Shaknon and Margath, a light came in his eyes, for they were wise and quiet, and watched the world, and something of their grandeur drew about him like a cloak. As age cut deep lines in his face and gave angles to his figure, a strange, settled dignity grew upon him, whether he swung his axe by the balsams or dressed the skins of the animals he had killed, piling up the pelts in a long shed in the stockade, a goodly heritage for his daughter, if she ever came back. Every day at sunrise he walked to the door of his house and looked eastward steadily, and sometimes there broke from his lips the words: "My daughter-Carille!" Again, he would sit and brood with his chin in his hand, and smile, as though remembering pleasant things.

One day at last, in the full tide of summer, a man, haggard and troubled, came to Felion's house, and knocked, and, getting no reply, waited; and whenever he looked down at the little city he wrung his hands, and more than once he put them up to his face and shuddered, and again looked for Felion. Just when the dusk was rolling down, Felion came back, and, seeing the man, would have passed him without a word, but that the man stopped with an eager, sorrowful gesture and said: "The plague has come upon us again, and the people, remembering how you healed them long ago, beg you to come."

At that Felion leaned his fishing-rod against the door and answered:

"What people?"

The other then replied: "The people of the little city below, Felion."

"I do not know your name," was the reply; "I know naught of you or of your city."

35

"Are you mad?" cried the man. "Do you forget the little city down there? Have you no heart?"

A strange smile passed over Felion's face, and he answered: "When one forgets, why should the other remember?"

He turned and went into the house and shut the door, and though the man knocked, the door was no opened, and he went back angry and miserable; and the people could not believe that Felion would no come to help them, as he had done all his life. A dawn three others came, and they found Felion looking out towards the east, his lips moving as though he prayed. Yet it was no prayer, only a call, that was on his lips. They felt a sort of awe in his presence, for now he seemed as if he had lived more than a century, so wise and old was the look of his face, so white his hair, so set and distant his dignity. They begged him to come, and, bringing his medicines, save the people, for death was galloping through the town, knocking at many doors.

"One came to heal you," he answered—"the young man of the schools, who wrote mystic letters after his name; it swings on a brass by his door-where is he?"

"He is dead of the plague," they replied, "and the other also that came with him, who fled before the sickness, fell dead of it on the roadside, going to the sea."

"Why should I go?" he replied, and he turned threateningly to his weapon, as if in menace of their presence.

"You have no one to leave behind," they answered eagerly, "and you are old."

"Liars," he rejoined, "let the little city save itself!" and he wheeled and went into his house, and they saw that they had erred in not remembering his daughter, whose presence they had once prized. They saw that they had angered him beyond soothing; and they went back in grief, for two of them had lost dear relatives by the fell sickness. When they told what had happened, the people said: "We will send the women; he will listen to them—he had a daughter."

That afternoon, when all the hills lay still and dead, and nowhere did bird or breeze stir, the women came, and they found him seated with his back turned to the town. He was looking into the deep woods, into the hot shadows of the trees.

36

"We have come to bring you to the little city," they said to him; "the sick grow in numbers every hour."

"It is safe in the hills," he answered, not looking at them. "Why do the people stay in the valley?"

"Every man has a friend, or a wife, or a child, ill or dying, and every woman has a husband, or a child, or a friend, or a brother. Cowards have fled, and many of them have fallen by the way."

"Last summer I lay sick here many weeks and none came near me—why should I go to the little city?" he demanded austerely. "Four times I saved it, and of all that I saved none came to give me water to drink, or food to eat, and I lay burning with fever, and thirsty and hungry—God of heaven, how thirsty!"

"We did not know," they answered humbly; "you came to us so seldom, we had forgotten; we were fools."

"I came and went fifty years," he answered bitterly, "and I have forgotten how to rid the little city of the plague!"

At that one of the women, mad with anger, made as if to catch him by his beard, but she forbore, and said: "Liar—the men shall hang you to your own rooftree!"

His eyes had a wild light, but he waved his hand quietly, and answered: "Begone, and learn how great a sin is ingratitude."

He turned away from them gloomily, and would have entered his home, but one of the women, who was young, plucked his sleeve, and said sorrowfully: "I loved Carille, your daughter."

"And forgot her and her father. I am three-score and ten years, and she has been gone fifteen, and for the first time I see your face," was his scornful reply.

She was tempted to say: "I was ever bearing children and nursing them, and the hills were hard to climb, and my husband would not go;" but she saw how dark his look was, and she hid her face in her hands and turned away to follow after the others. She had five little children, and her heart was anxious for them and her eyes full of tears.

Anger and remorse seized on the little city, and there were those who would have killed Felion, but others saw that the old man had been sorely wronged in the past, and these said: "Wait until the morrow and we will devise something."

That night a mule-train crept slowly down the mountain side and entered the little city, for no one who came with them knew of the plague. The caravan had come from the east across the great plains, and not from the west, which was the travelled highway to the sea. Among them was a woman who already was ill of a fever, and knew naught of what passed round her. She had with her a beautiful child; and one of the women of the place devised a thing. "This woman," she said, "does not belong to the little city, and he can have nothing against her; she is a stranger. Let one of us take this beautiful lad to him, and he shall ask Felion to come and save his mother."

Every one approved the woman's wisdom, and in the early morning she herself, with another, took the child and went up the long hillside in the heavy heat; and when they came near Felion's house the women stayed behind, and the child went forward, having been taught what to say to the old man.

Felion sat just within his doorway, looking out into the sunlight which fell upon the red and white walls of the little city, flanked by young orchards, with great, oozy meadows beyond these, where cattle ate, knee-deep in the lush grass and cool reed-beds. Along the riverside, far up on the high banks, were the tall couches of dead Indians, set on poles, their useless weapons laid along the deerskin pall. Down the hurrying river there passed a raft, bearing a black flag on a pole, and on it were women and children who were being taken down to the sea from the doomed city. These were they who had lost fathers and brothers; and now were going out alone with the shadow of the plague over them, for there was none to say them nay. The tall oarsmen bent to their task, and Felion felt his blood beat faster when he saw the huge oars swing high, then drop and bend in the water, as the raft swung straight in its course and passed on safe through the narrow slide into the white rapids below, which licked the long timbers as with white tongues, and tossed spray upon the sad voyagers. Felion remembered the day when he left his own child behind and sprang from the bridge to the raft whereon were the children of the little city, and saved them.

And when he tried to be angry now, the thought of the children as they watched him, with his broken leg striving against their peril, softened his heart. He shook his head, for suddenly there came to him the memory of a time, three-score years before, when he and the foundryman's daughter had gone hunting flag-flowers by the little trout stream; of the songs they sang together at the festivals, she in her sweet Quaker garb and demure Quaker beauty, he lithe, alert, and full of the joy of life and loving. As he sat so, thinking, he wondered where she was, and why he should be thinking of her now, facing the dreary sorrow of this pestilence and his own anger and vengeance. He nodded softly to the waving trees far down in the valley, for his thoughts had drifted on to his wife as he first saw her. She was standing bare-armed among the grape-vines by a wall of rock, the dew of rich life on her lip and forehead, her grey eyes swimming with a soft light; and looking at her he had loved her at once, as he had loved, on the instant, the little child that came to him later; as he had loved the girl into which the child grew, till she left him and came back no more. Why had he never gone in search of her?

He got to his feet involuntarily and stepped towards the door, looking down into the valley. As his eyes rested on the little city his face grew dark, but his eyes were troubled and presently grew bewildered, for out of a green covert near there stepped a pretty boy, who came to him with frank, unabashed face and a half-shy smile.

Felion did not speak at first, but stood looking, and presently the child said: "I have come to fetch you."

"To fetch me where, little man?" asked Felion, a light coming into his face, his heart beating faster.

"To my mother. She is sick."

"Where is your mother?"

"She's in the village down there," answered the boy, pointing.

In spite of himself, Felion smiled in a sour sort of way, for the boy had called the place a village, and he relished the unconscious irony.

"What is the matter with her?" asked Felion, beckoning the lad inside.

The lad came and stood in the doorway, gazing round curiously, while the old man sat down and looked at him, moved, he knew not why.

The bright steel of Felion's axe, standing in the corner, caught the lad's eye and held it. Felion saw, and said: "What are you thinking of?"

The lad answered: "Of the axe. When I'm bigger I will cut down trees and build a house, a bridge, and a city. Aren't you coming quick to help my mother? She will die if you don't come."

Felion did not answer, and from the trees without two women watched him anxiously.

"Why should I come?" asked Felion curiously. "Because she's sick, and she's my mother."

"Why should I do it because she's your mother?"

"I don't know," the lad answered, and his brow knitted in the attempt to think it out, "but I like you." He came and stood beside the old man and looked into his face with a pleasant confidence. "If your mother was sick, and I could heal her, I would—I know I would—I wouldn't be afraid to go down into the village."

Here were rebuke, love, and impeachment, all in one, and the old man half started from his seat.

"Did you think I was afraid?" he asked of the boy, as simply as might a child of a child, so near are children and wise men in their thoughts.

"I knew if you didn't it'd be because you were angry or were afraid, and you didn't look angry."

"How does one look when one is angry?"

"Like my father."

"And how does your father look?"

"My father's dead."

"Did he die of the plague?" asked Felion, laying his hand on the lad's shoulder.

"No," said the lad quickly, and shut his lips tight.

"Won't you tell me?" asked Felion, with a strange inquisitiveness.

"No. Mother'll tell you, but I won't." The lad's eyes filled with tears.

"Poor boy—poor boy!" said Felion, and his hand tightened on the small shoulder.

40

"Don't be sorry for me; be sorry for mother, please," said the boy, and he laid a hand on the old man's knee, and that touch went to a heart long closed against the little city below; and Felion rose and said: "I will go with you to your mother."

Then he went into another room, and the boy came near the axe and ran his fingers along the bright steel, and fondled the handle, as does a hunter the tried weapon which has been his through many seasons. When the old man came back he said to the boy: "Why do you look at the axe?"

"I don't know," was the answer; "maybe because my mother used to sing a song about the wood-cutters." Without a word, and thinking much, he stepped out into the path leading to the little city, the lad holding one hand. Years afterwards men spoke with a sort of awe or reverence of seeing the beautiful stranger lad leading old Felion into the plague-stricken place, and how, as they passed, women threw themselves at Felion's feet, begging him to save their loved ones. And a drunkard cast his arm round the old man's shoulder and sputtered foolish pleadings in his ear; but Felion only waved them back gently, and said: "By-and-by, by-and-by—God help us all!"

Now a fevered hand snatched at him from a doorway, moanings came from everywhere, and more than once he almost stumbled over a dead body; others he saw being carried away to the graveyard for hasty burial. Few were the mourners that followed, and the faces of those who watched the processions go by were set and drawn. The sunlight and the green trees seemed an insult to the dead.

They passed into the house where the sick woman lay, and some met him at the door with faces of joy and meaning; for now they knew the woman and would have spoken to him of her; but he waved them off, and put his fingers upon his lips and went where a fire burned in a kitchen, and brewed his medicines. And the child entered the room where his mother lay, and presently he came to the kitchen and said: "She is asleep—my mother."

The old man looked down on him a moment steadily, and a look of bewilderment came into his face. But he turned away again to the simmering pots. The boy went to the window and, leaning upon the sill, began to hum softly a sort of chant, while he watched a lizard running hither and thither in the sun. As he hummed, the old man listened, and presently, with his medicines in his hands and a half-startled look, he came over to the lad. "What are you humming?" he asked.

41

The lad answered: "A song of the wood-cutters."
"Sing it again," said Felion.
The lad began to sing:
  "Here shall I build me my cedar house,
  A city with gates, a road to the sea—
  For I am the lord of the Earth! Hew! Hew!"
The old man stopped him. "What is your name?"

"My name is Felion," answered the lad; and he put his face close to the jug that held the steaming tinctures: but the old man caught the little chin in his huge hand and bent back the head, looking long into the lad's eyes. At last he caught little Felion's hand and hurried into the other room, where the woman lay in a stupor. The old man came quickly to her and looked into her face. Seeing, he gave a broken cry and said:

"Carille, my daughter! Carille!"

He drew her to his breast, and as he did so he groaned aloud, for he knew that inevitable Death was waiting for her at the door. He straightened himself up, clasped the child to his breast, and said: "I, too, am Felion, my little son."

And then he set about to defeat that dark, hovering Figure at the door.

For three long hours he sat beside her, giving her little by little his potent medicines; and now and again he stopped his mouth with his hand, lest he should cry out; and his eyes never wavered from her face, not even to the boy, who lay asleep in the corner.

At last his look relaxed its vigilance, for a dewy look passed over the woman's face, and she opened her eyes and saw him, and gave a little cry of "Father!" and was straightway lost in his arms.

"I have come home to die," she said.

"No, no, to live!" he answered firmly. "Why did you not send me word all these long years?"

"My husband was in shame, in prison, and I in sorrow," she answered sadly. "I could not."

"He did evil? He is—" he paused.

42

"He is dead," she said. "It is better so." Her eyes wandered round the room restlessly, and then fixed upon the sleeping child, and a smile passed over her face. She pointed to the lad.

The old man nodded. "He brought me here," he said gently. Then he got to his feet. "You must sleep now," he added, and he gave her a cordial. "I must go forth and save the sick."

"Is it a plague?" she asked.

He nodded. "They said you would not come to save them," she continued reproachfully. "You came to me because I was your Carille, only for that?"

"No, no," he answered; "I knew not who you were. I came to save a mother to her child."

"Thank God!" she said.

With a happy smile she hid her face in the pillow. At last, leaving her and the child asleep, old Felion went forth into the little city, and the people flocked to him, and for many days he came and went ceaselessly.

And once more he saved the city, and the people blessed him: and the years go on.

THE FORGE IN THE VALLEY

He lay where he could see her working at the forge. As she worked she sang:
"When God was making the world,
(Swift is the wind and white is the fire)
The feet of his people danced the stars;
There was laughter and swinging bells,

And clanging iron and breaking breath,
The hammers of heaven making the hills,
The vales on the anvil of God.
(Wild is the fire and low is the wind.)"

His eyes were shining, and his face had a pale radiance from the reflected light, though he lay in the shadow where he could watch her, while she could not see him. Now her hand was upon the bellows, and the low, white fire seethed hungrily up, and set its teeth upon the iron she held; now it turned the iron about upon the anvil, and the sparks showered about her very softly and strangely. There was a cheerful gravity in her motions, a high, fine look in her face.

They two lived alone in the solitudes of Megalon Valley.

It was night now, and the pleasant gloom of the valley was not broken by any sound save the hum of the stream nearby, and the song, and the ringing anvil. But into the workshop came the moist, fragrant smell of the acacia and the maple, and a long brown lizard stretched its neck sleepily across the threshold of the door opening into the valley.

The song went on:
"When God had finished the world
(Bright was the fire and sweet was the wind)
Up from the valleys came song,
To answer the morning stars,
And the hand of man on the anvil rang;
His breath was big in his breast, his life
Beat strong on the walls of the world.
(Glad is the wind and tall is the fire.)"

He put his hands to his eyes, and took them away again, as though to make sure that the song was not a dream. Wonder grew upon his thin, bearded face, he ran his fingers through his thick hair in a dazed way. Then he lay and looked, and a rich warm flush crept over his cheek, and stayed there.

There was a great gap in his memory.

The evening wore on. Once or twice the woman turned towards the room where the man lay, and listened—she could not see his face from where she stood. At such times he lay still, though his heart beat quickly, like that of an expectant child. His lips opened to speak, but still they remained silent. As yet he was like a returned traveller who does not quickly recognise old familiar things, and who is struggling with vague suggestions and forgotten events. As time went on, the woman turned towards the doorway oftener, and shifted her position so that she faced it, and the sparks, flying up, lighted her face with a wonderful irregular brightness.

"Samantha," he said at last, and his voice sounded so strange to him that the word quivered timidly towards her.

She paused upon a stroke, and some new note in his voice sent so sudden a thrill to her heart that she caught her breath with a painful kind of joy. The hammer dropped upon the anvil, and, in a moment, she stood in the doorway of his room.

"Francis, Francis," she responded in a low whisper. He started up from his couch of skins. "Samantha, my wife!" he cried, in a strong proud voice.

She dropped beside him and caught his head, like a mother, to her shoulder, and set her warm lips on his forehead and hair with a kind of hunger; and then he drew her face down and kissed her on the lips. Tears hung at her eyes, and presently dropped on her cheeks, a sob shook her, and then she was still, her hands grasping his shoulders.

"Have I been ill?" he asked.

"You have been very ill, Francis."

"Has it been long?"

Her fingers passed tenderly through his grizzled hair. "Too long, too long, my husband," she replied.

"Is it summer now?"

45

"Yes, Francis, it is summer."

"Was it in the spring, Samantha?—Yes, I think it was in the spring," he added, musing.

"It was in a spring."

"There was snow still on the mountain-top, the river was running high, and wild fowl were gathered on the island in the lake—yes, I remember, I think."

"And the men were working at the mine," she whispered, her voice shaking a little, and her eyes eagerly questioning his face.

"Ah, the mine—it was the mine, Samantha!" he said abruptly, his eyes flashing up. "I was working at the forge to make a great bolt for the machinery, and some one forgot and set the engine in motion. I ran out; but it was too late... and then..."

"And then you tried to save them, Francis, and you were hurt."

"What month is this, my wife?"

"It is December."

"And that was in October?"

"Yes, in October."

"I have been ill since? What happened?"

"Many were killed, Francis, and you and I came away."

"Where are we now? I do not know the place."

"This is Megalon Valley. You and I live alone here."

"Why did you bring me here?"

"I did not bring you, Francis; you wished me to come. One day you said to me: 'There is a place in Megalon Valley where, long ago, an old man lived, who had become a stranger among men—a place where the blackbird stays, and the wolf-dog troops and hides, and the damson grows as thick as blossoms on the acacia. We will go there.' And I came with you."

"I do not remember. What of the mine? Was I a coward and left the mine? There was no one understood the ways of the wheel, and rod, and steam, save me.

"The mine is closed, Francis," she answered gently. "You were no coward, but— but you had strange fancies.

"When did the mine close?" he said, with a kind of sorrow; "I put hard work and good years into it." At that moment, when her face drew close to his, the vision of her as she stood at the anvil came to him with a new impression, and he said again in a half-frightened way: "When did it close, Samantha?"

"The mine was closed—twelve years ago, my own dear husband."

He got to his feet and clasped her to his breast. A strength came to him which had eluded him twelve years, and she, womanlike, delighted in that strength, and, with a great gladness, changed eyes and hands with him; keeping her soul still her own, brooding and lofty, as is the soul of every true woman, though, like this one, she labours at a forge, and in a far, untenanted country is faithful friend, ceaseless apothecary to a comrade with a disordered mind; living on savage meats, clothing herself and the other in skins, and, with a divine persistence, keeping a cheerful heart, certain that the intelligence which was frightened from its home would come back one day. It should be hers to watch for the great moment, and give the wanderer loving welcome, lest it should hurry madly away again into the desert, never to return.

She had her reward, yet she wept. She had carried herself before him with the bright ways of an unvexed girl these twelve years past; she had earned the salt of her tears. He was dazed still, but, the doublet of his mind no longer unbraced, he understood what she had been to him, and how she had tended him in absolute loneliness, her companions the wild things of the valley—these and God.

He drew her into the workshop, and put his hand upon the bellows and churned them, so that the fire roared joyously up, and the place was red with the light. In this light he turned her to him and looked at her. The look was as that of one who had come back from the dead—that naked, profound, unconditional gaze which is as deep and honest as the primeval sense. His eyes fell upon her rich, firm, stately body; it lingered for a moment on the brown fulness of her hair; then her look was gathered to his, and they fell into each other's arms.

For long they sat in the solemn silence of their joy, and so awed were they by the thing which had come to them that they felt no surprise when a wolf-dog crawled over the lizard on the threshold, and stole along the wall with shining, bloody eyes to an inner room, and stayed there munching meat to surfeit and drowsiness, and at last crept out and lay beside the forge in a thick sleep. These two had lived so much with the untamed things of nature, the bellows and the fire had been so long there, and the clang of the anvil was so familiar, that there was a kinship among them, man and beast, with the woman as ruler.

"Tell me, Samantha," he said at last, "what has happened during these twelve years, all from the first. Keep nothing back. I am strong now." He looked around the workshop, then, suddenly, at her, with a strange pain, and they both turned their heads away for an instant, for the same thought was on them. Then, presently, she spoke, and answered his shy, sorrowful thought before all else. "The child is gone," she softly said.

He sat still, but a sob was in his throat. He looked at her with a kind of fear. He wondered if his madness had cost the life of the child. She understood. "Did I ever see the child?" he asked.

"Oh yes, I sometimes thought that through the babe you would be yourself again. When you were near her you never ceased to look at her and fondle her, as I thought very timidly; and you would start sometimes and gaze at me with the old wise look hovering at your eyes. But the look did not stay. The child was fond of you, but she faded and pined, and one day as you nursed her you came to me and said: 'See, beloved, the little one will not wake. She pulled at my beard and said, "Daddy," and fell asleep.' And I took her from your arms.... There is a chestnut tree near the door of our cottage at the mine. One night you and I buried her there; but you do not remember her, do you?"

"My child, my child!" he said, looking out into the night; and he lifted up his arms and looked at them. "I held her here, and still I never held her; I fondled her, and yet I never fondled her; I buried her, yet—to me—she never was born."

"You have been far away, Francis; you have come back home. I waited, and prayed, and worked with you, and was patient.... It is very strange," she continued. "In all these twelve years you cannot remember our past, though you remembered about this place—the one thing, as if God had made it so— and now you cannot remember those twelve years."

"Tell me now of the twelve years," he urged.

"It was the same from day to day. When we came from the mountain, we brought with us the implements of the forge upon a horse. Now and again as we travelled we cut our way through the heavy woods. You were changed for the better then; a dreadful trouble seemed to have gone from your face. There was a strong kind of peace in the valley, and there were so many birds and animals, and the smell of the trees was so fine, that we were not lonely, neither you nor I."

She paused, thinking, her eyes looking out to where the Evening Star was sailing slowly out of the wooded horizon, his look on her. In the pause the wolf-dog raised its big, sleepy eyes at them, then plunged its head into its paws, its wildness undisturbed by their presence.

Presently the wife continued: "At last we reached here, and here we have lived, where no human being, save one, has ever been. We put up the forge, and in a little hill not far away we found coal for it. The days went on. It was always summer, though there came at times a sharp frost, and covered the ground with a coverlet of white. But the birds were always with us, and the beasts were our friends. I learned to love even the shrill cry of the reed hens, and the soft tap-tap of the wood-pecker is the sweetest music to my ear after the song of the anvil. How often have you and I stood here at the anvil, the fire heating the iron, and our hammers falling constantly! Oh, Francis, I knew that only here with God and His dumb creatures, and His wonderful healing world, all sun, and wind, and flowers, and blossoming trees, working as you used to work, as the first of men worked, would the sane wandering soul return to you. The thought was in you, too, for you led me here, and have been patient also in the awful exile of your mind."

"I have been as a child, and not as a man," he said gravely. "Shall I ever again be a man, as I once was, Samantha?"

"You cannot see yourself," she said. "A week ago you fell ill, and since then you have been pale and worn; but your body has been, and is, that of a great strong man. In the morning I will take you to a spring in the hills, and you shall see yourself, beloved."

He stood up, stretched himself, went to the door, and looked out into the valley flooded with moonlight. He drew in a great draught of air, and said: "The world—the great, wonderful world, where men live, and love work, and do strong things!"—he paused, and turned with a trouble in his face. "My wife," he said, "you have lived with a dead man twelve years, and I have lost twelve years in the world. I had a great thought once—an invention—but now—" he hung his head bitterly. She came to him, and her hands slid up along his breast to his shoulders, and rested there; and she said, with a glad smile: "Francis, you have lost nothing. The thing—the invention—was all but finished when you fell ill a week ago. We have worked at it for these twelve years; through it, I think, you have been brought back to me. Come, there is a little work yet to, do upon it;" and she drew him to where a machine of iron lay in the corner. With a great cry he fell upon his knees beside it, and fondled it.

Then, presently, he rose, and caught his wife to his breast.

Together, a moment later, they stood beside the anvil. The wolf-dog fled out into the night from the shower of sparks, as, in the red light, the two sang to the clanging of the hammers:

"When God was making the world

(Swift is the wind and white is the fire)"